I love you Dippy Lippy:
a forever promise

By Michelle Lee Graham

I Love You Dippy Lippy: A Forever Promise

Editor: Alexa Tanen

Illustrator: Yelyzaveta Serdyuk

Format: Rocio Monroy

Photographer: Jacqui Banta

This book is dedicated to my strong and creative daughter, Rachel Ross. You have taught me how to love deeper than I ever knew I could! Your life and love has made me a better person and a proud mom. I love you Dippy Lippy will forever be our special promise! You fill my heart with unwavering love!

The clock read 8:00 pm, bedtime for Rachel.
Time to begin our nightly routine of tuck-ins,
stories, and prayers. Rachel snuggled into her
warm blankets, her beautiful blue eyes peeking
over the top, "Mommy, will you tell me again
how much you love me?"

4

This was often part of our nightly routine. Before Rachel could even finish the question, I had already stretched my arms as far as they could go. "I love you as much as all the fish in the ocean and all the birds in the sky!" Rachel replied, "I love you as much as all the stars in the universe."

5

We both giggled, and I tucked the blankets tightly around her little body. I leaned down and whispered in her ear, "And I love you even more than all of that." She smiled quietly and closed her eyes to sleep. As the years went by; we never grew tired of our nightly routine. Rachel and I would share how much we loved each other in fun and imaginative ways.

The clock read 8:00 pm, bedtime for Rachel. Time to begin our nightly routine of tuck-ins, stories, and prayers. Rachel started, "I love you as much as all the grains of sand on the beach." I followed with, "I love you as much as all the grains of sand on the beach and all the leaves in the trees!"

7

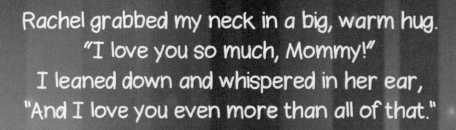

Rachel grabbed my neck in a big, warm hug.
"I love you so much, Mommy!"
I leaned down and whispered in her ear,
"And I love you even more than all of that."

The clock read 8:00 pm, bedtime for Rachel. I began this time,
"I love you as much as all the strands of grass in all the fields."
Rachel stayed quiet, so I added more.
"And as high as the tallest mountain..."
She was still quiet.

"As much as all the tickles by all the moms and dads."
I tickled the sides of her tummy as she giggled. As I tucked the
blankets around her little body Rachel finally replied,
"Mommy, I wish there was a word that was bigger than everything.
A word that is the biggest of all the other words and that nothing
could be more because that's how much I love you!"

I smiled gently and brushed my hand across her cheek.
I thought quietly for a moment. Then I had an idea.

"What if we make up our
own word? A word that means
the biggest of all things?
It could be anything we want,
and it will be our own
special word."

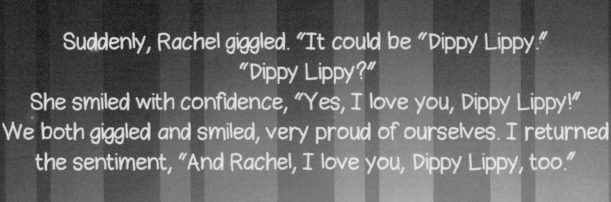

Suddenly, Rachel giggled. "It could be "Dippy Lippy."
"Dippy Lippy?"
She smiled with confidence, "Yes, I love you, Dippy Lippy!"
We both giggled and smiled, very proud of ourselves. I returned
the sentiment, "And Rachel, I love you, Dippy Lippy, too."

12

I kissed the top of her nose.
Rachel laid in her bed with a smile from ear to ear.
We knew we had created something special.

The following night, we talked more about Dippy Lippy.
We were excited to have our own word. We agreed that nothing
could be bigger, stronger, taller, or more than Dippy Lippy.
There could not be more than one
Dippy Lippy because it was already
the "Most and Biggest" all by itself.

As the years went by, bedtime always included tuck-ins, stories, prayers, and of course, Dippy Lippy.

One day, when Rachel was nine years old,
I asked her if she had any homework.
She assured me that she did not.
I was not sure that I believed her.

16

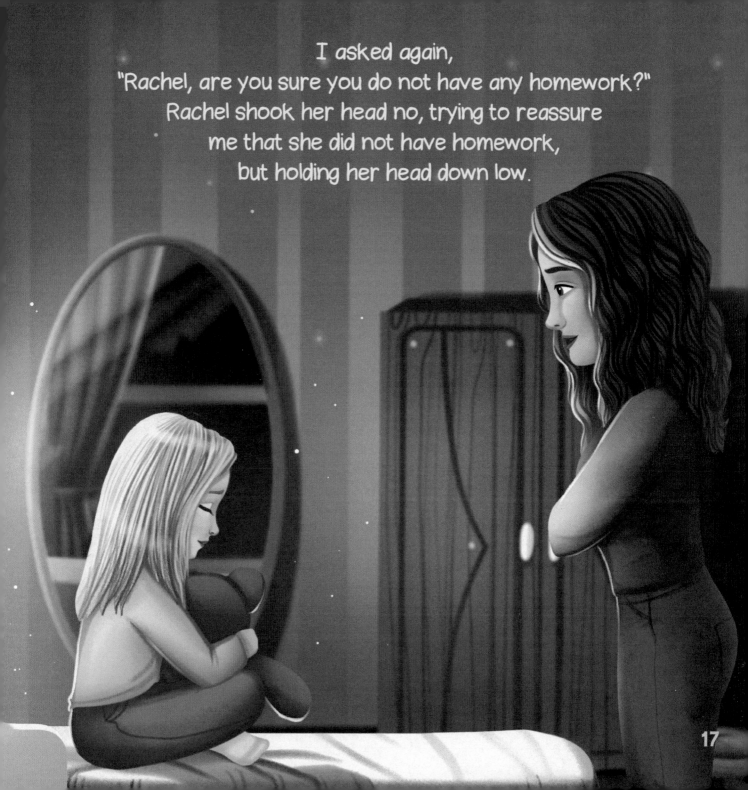

I asked again,
"Rachel, are you sure you do not have any homework?"
Rachel shook her head no, trying to reassure
me that she did not have homework,
but holding her head down low.

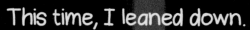

This time, I leaned down.
"Rachel, do you Dippy Lippy promise that you do not have homework?"
Rachel looked up at me quickly. We had never said that before.
Her bright blue eyes began to fill with tears.
"I am sorry Mommy; I will go do my homework."

18

From that day on, Dippy Lippy became more to us than our expression of how much we loved each other, it became our promise in every situation when it was needed.

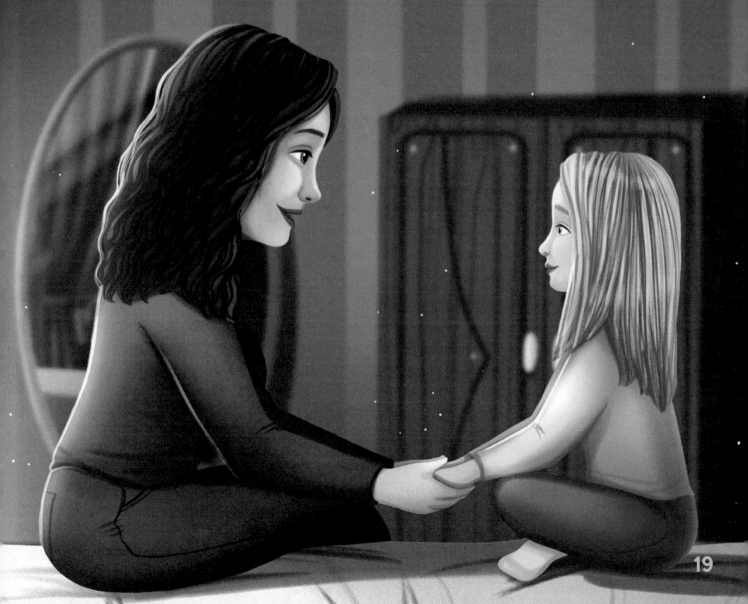

As the years went by, Rachel became a teenager, but I would still come to her room at nighttime. I'd ask how her day was, and sometimes, I would say, "Hey Rach, I love you, Dippy Lippy."

She would smile. In some ways, she loved it. In other ways, she did not. It was silly, now that she was a cool teenager. Nevertheless, she would reply, "I love you too, Mom," and sometimes she would add, "Dippy Lippy."

21

More years went by, and Rachel graduated from High School. On her graduation day, I was so very proud of her.

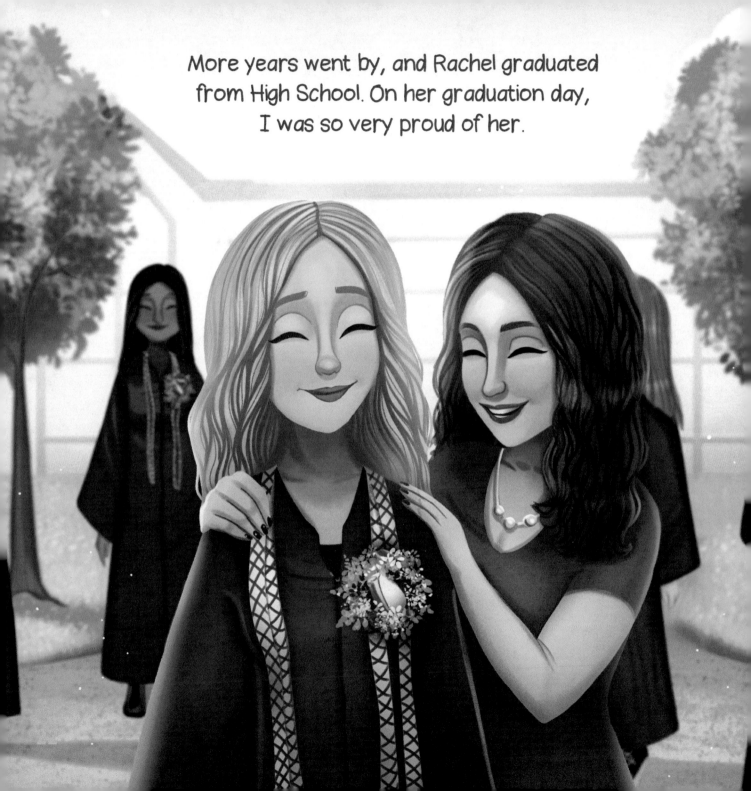

I sat down to write her a letter to express how much I loved her. I wrote a long letter about her great choices and dedication to school. I tried to say everything I could think of, but I kept finding myself with not enough words to express my love and pride. Suddenly it dawned on me. "I love you, Dippy Lippy!"

After that, Rachel moved away to go to college.
I missed her so much. I wondered if she was having fun, was
staying safe, and if she thought of me as much as I thought of her.

As I was lying in bed one night, thinking about my girl,
I received a text. With only a few words, she brightened my mood.
"I love you, Dippy Lippy Mama."
I laid there and smiled from ear to ear.

More years went by,
and Rachel now had a husband,
children, and a house of her own.

26

I had lived a good life but was getting much older and weaker.

One day, Rachel called. She talked about her busy life,
her job, the kids, and the projects she was working on.
I loved to hear all about it. When it was my turn to talk,
I cleared my throat. "I am doing just fine."
I wasn't telling the whole truth:
I was fragile and sick.

"Mom, are you ok?"

"Yes, of course," I lied.

"Mom, Dippy Lippy promise, are you ok?"

With tears in my eyes, I knew I had to tell the truth. I was very sick and would not live much longer. I asked Rachel to make me one last Dippy Lippy promise. With tears rolling down her cheeks, she promised me.

29

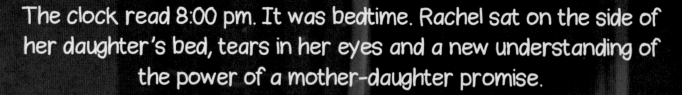

The clock read 8:00 pm. It was bedtime. Rachel sat on the side of her daughter's bed, tears in her eyes and a new understanding of the power of a mother-daughter promise.

Rachel leaned down and whispered to her precious girl. "I love you, Dippy Lippy."

The End

ABOUT THE AUTHOR

Michelle Lee Graham is a dynamic author and inspirational CEO. Her vulnerability helps her deliver authentic, multifaceted motivation. Michelle finds fulfillment in motherhood with her five amazing children. Her successful career and family continuously inspire Michelle to share her story with others.

Michelle Lee
Graham

http://michelleleegraham.com/

OTHER TITLES BY MICHELLE :

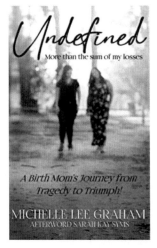

All books are available in Spanish

Available on

Scan the code to get your own copy